ONE NIGHT HE covered the window and door of their whare with cloaks and mats to block out early morning light.

Taranga overslept and Maui saw her hurry out into the sunrise.

DOWN THE HILL from the pa she raced.

Maui, following behind, saw her leap into a hole and disappear from sight.

HE PEERED INTO the hole.
He dropped sticks and stones, but could not hear them land.
'If my mother can do it, so can I,' thought Maui, and he sprang after her.

AS HE FELL, he chanted the karakia to turn himself into Rupe, the wood-pigeon. With a flutter of his wings he flopped into a pile of bracken at the bottom of the hole.

HE CREPT ALONG the tunnel that led from the hole until it opened onto a vast underground land.
Beneath a tree he could see his mother and a man.
Could this man be his father?

MAUI FLUTTERED INTO the branches of the puriri tree.
He plucked a berry and dropped it on the man.
The man looked up and Maui dropped another.

THE MAN JUMPED up in anger.

He called to other people of the underworld, and they began to throw stones at the cheeky pigeon.

MAUI SKILFULLY DODGED the people's stones, but when the man flung one he let it hit him on his feathered chest.
He pitched from the tree and flopped at the man's feet.

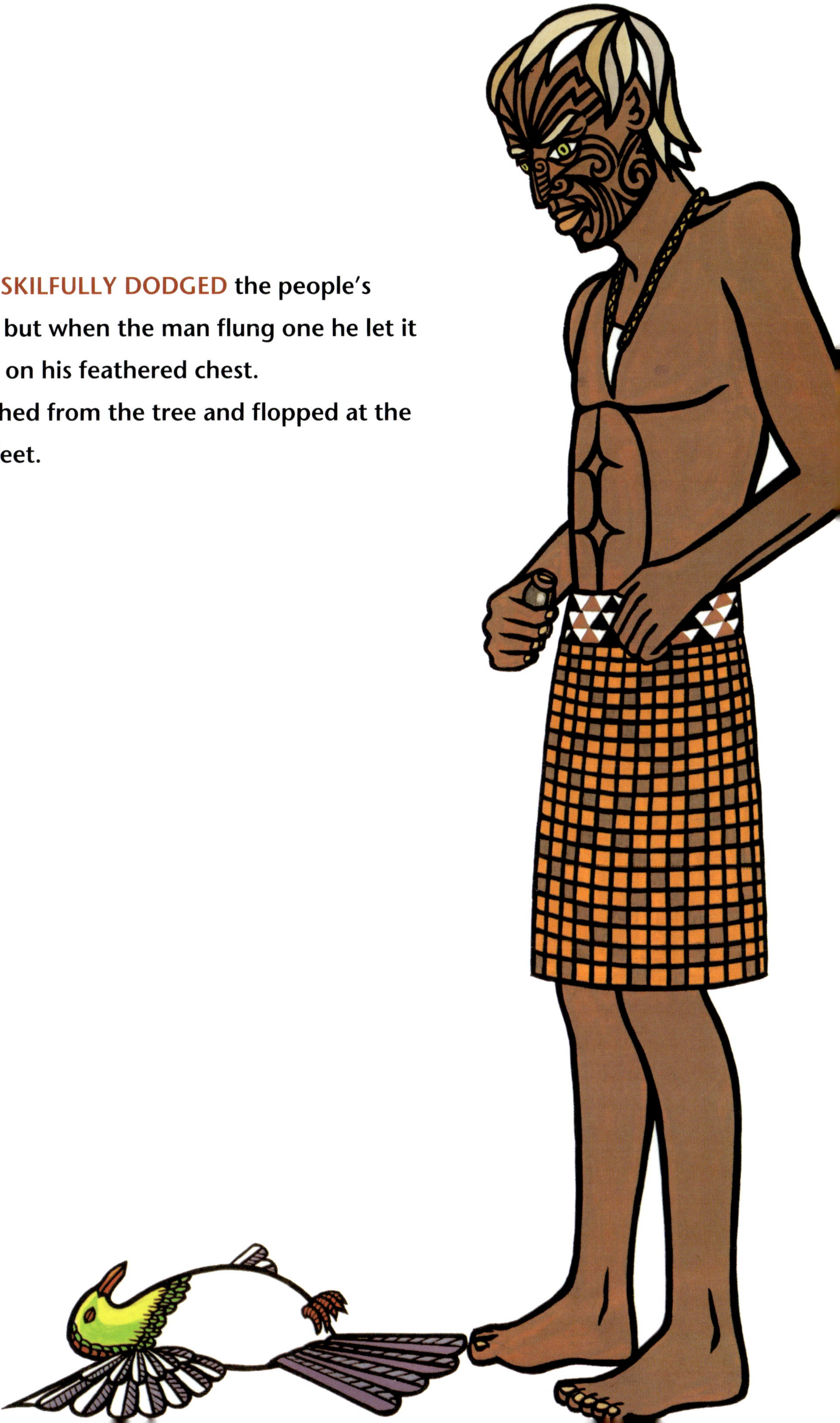

AS THE MAN bent to pick him up, Maui sprang to his feet in his human form. Then they knew that they were father and son.

MAUI'S FATHER, WHOSE name was Makea-tutara, took his son to a sacred waterfall and bathed him in its waters. He chanted karakia to give Maui more magical powers and everlasting life.

MAUI WAS HAPPY. He had found his father.
But Makea-tutara was sad.
He had made a mistake when chanting the karakia over Maui.
It was only a little slip, but he knew it would one day cost Maui his life.

MAUI'S GRANDFATHER, MURI-RANGI-WHENUA, lived in the underworld too, and each day Maui would bring him his food.
One day he hid it, and his grandfather asked, 'Where is my kai, Maui?'
'Give me your magic jawbone and I will give you your kai,' said Maui.
'No!' said his grandfather.
So every day Maui would hide his food and ask him again.

AT LAST MURI-RANGI-WHENUA became too hungry and he gave in.
He slipped his magic jawbone from his mouth and gave it to Maui.
'Tame the Sun with this bone, Maui,' he said.
'Find the Secret of Fire and fish up a land.
But do not defy Hine, the Goddess of Death, or you will surely die.'

MAUI FELT THE power of the bone course through him.

'I will tame the Sun!'

'I will find the Secret of Fire!'

'I will even defy Death!'

AND WHEN HE returned from the underworld to the land above, he did. But that is another story.